FIRST
ILLUSTRATED CLASSICS

Black Beauty

Anna Sewell

Retold by Jenny J. Hunter
Illustrated by Barry Davies

Contents

Grazing peacefully at his mother's side in the cool, green meadow, the handsome, young colt, Black Beauty, could never have imagined the events that were to take place as he grew older. Black Beauty tells his own story . . . a story of kind and gentle masters who loved him well and others who were cruel and uncaring. We learn about life in the country and in the city and of things that happened to Black Beauty and his friends. His story shows that horses have feelings too, sometimes knowing more than we realise and that, well-treated, they will remain our true and loyal friends.

Chapter 1
My First Happy Years

As I look back, my earliest memories are of a huge, grass field with a tiny pond. The pond was shaded by leafy, green trees and beautiful water lilies floated on the water.

When I was a young foal I drank my mother's milk because I was not old enough to eat grass. I ran beside her during the day and at night I slept at her side.

When it was warm weather we would stand in the shade of the trees, by the pond.

During the winter we would go to a warm shed beside the apple orchard.

Six other colts were in the field with me. I was younger than all of them. Some were nearly as big as fully-grown horses. It was fun to run and play with them. At times we used to kick and bite each other.

Once when there was rather a lot of kicking my mother called to me to come to her side and said,

"I trust you will grow up kind and gentle and learn no bad habits. Always work your hardest. When you trot, pick up your feet, and do not kick or bite, even if it is in play."

I always remembered my mother's words. I knew she was very wise and that she was loved by our master. He usually called her Pet, although her name was Duchess.

Our master was a kind man. We had a good home with good food and plenty of kind words. We all loved our master and he would talk to us as if we were his children. My mother would whinny when she saw him and

run to the gate to meet him. As he stroked and patted her he would say,

"Now, my Pet, how is little 'Blackie'?" My coat was black so he called me 'Blackie'. Then he would give my mother a carrot and me a piece of bread. The other horses would all come to him, but I'm sure we were his favourites. On market day, it was always my mother who took him to the town in a small carriage.

From time to time a young boy called Dick came into our field to pick blackberries from the bushes. When he had eaten as much as he wanted he thought it was fun to throw sticks and stones at the horses. But when we were hit by the stones it was very painful.

One day when Dick was throwing stones at us, he did not realise that my master was nearby and could see what was happening. When he saw Dick throw a stone he ran and held him by the arm. Then my master hit

Dick's ears so hard that the boy cried out in surprise and pain. When we saw the master we raced up closer to see what was happening. "Wicked boy!" he said, "wicked boy to hurt the colts! This may not be the first time, but it will certainly be the last. Here is your money – now go. I never want to see you on my farm again."

Now that Dick had gone forever, old Daniel came to look after us. He was as kind and gentle as our master, so we were lucky horses.

Chapter 2
There is Much for Me to Learn

I was becoming a handsome, young horse. My deep black coat was fine and soft. There was a pretty, white star on my forehead and I had one white foot. Everyone seemed to like me but, until I was four years old, my master would not sell me. He said that just as boys should not do the work of men, colts should not do the work of fully-grown horses.

Squire Gordon came to see me when I was four years old. He inspected my mouth, eyes and legs. Then he watched as I walked, trotted and galloped. He appeared to like me and said, "He will be just right, once he has been broken in."

I was to be broken in by my master himself. He wanted to make sure that I was not frightened or hurt. My master said he would start the next day.

Some people may not know what breaking in is, so I will explain. When horses are broken in, they are taught to wear a saddle and bridle and to carry a rider on their back. They are also taught how to behave when pulling a cart. They must go at the speed the driver wishes and they must learn never to rear up or to kick or bite.

Even when hungry or tired, a good horse will always obey his master. All the time his harness is on, he must be calm and quiet and he cannot leap about or lie down to rest. So you can understand that it is not an easy thing for a horse to be broken in.

I had become used to wearing a halter and

a headcollar, but now I must get used to a bridle and bit. As was usual, my master gave me some oats and, after a lot of persuading, he managed to get the bit into my mouth and the bridle in position. It was a dreadful thing!

It hurt my mouth a lot. You cannot begin to know how it feels unless you have had a bit in your mouth. A piece of cold, hard steel is pushed into the mouth. It is as thick as a man's finger and goes over the tongue, between the teeth and the ends come out at the corners of the mouth. The bit is held in place by leather straps which go over the head, around the nose and under the chin; another strap is fastened under the chin, and it is impossible to get rid of the horrible thing. However, I knew that adult horses all wore bits and that my mother always had a bit in her mouth when she went out. My master was patient and gently coaxed me until at last I learned how to wear my bridle and bit.

Next came the saddle which was not quite so bad. Old Daniel held my head while my master put the saddle on my back very gently. He patted me and talked quietly to me as he fastened it on and then he gave me some oats. This happened every day and I soon got used to wearing the saddle.

Then it was time for my master to ride me. He sat on my back as I walked around the field. How strange it felt, but I was happy and proud to carry my master.

Learning to have iron shoes put on my feet was very hard at first. To make sure that I was not frightened or hurt, my master went with me to the blacksmith's shop. The blacksmith held up each one of my feet to cut off part of the hoof. It did not hurt, so I stood quietly on three legs until he had finished them all. Next came the shoes; the iron had been shaped to fit my feet.

The blacksmith hammered some nails

through each shoe and into my hoof. This was to fasten the shoes firmly on my feet. At first my feet felt heavy and stiff but I soon got used to having shoes on. The next thing I had to get used to was a harness. My master put the heavy collar on my neck and a bridle, which had large side pieces called blinkers, fitted against my eyes. I could only see straight in front of me when I had them on. A very stiff strap, called the crupper, fitted right under my tail and I hated this. My tail had to be doubled up to push it through the strap and it made me want to jump and kick, but I would never do such a thing because I loved my master very much. My kind master let me have a holiday for two weeks. He put me in a field which was near the railway tracks. At first, I was terrified when I heard and saw a train and I raced away as fast as I could, but before long I got used to the trains.

Since then, I have seen many horses so

frightened at the sight of a train that they have thrown their riders and run away. But (thanks to my early training) I am fearless at railway stations.

On many occasions my master drove me in double harness with my mother. She was experienced and wise and I could learn from her. She told me that I should be sensible and try to please my master because if I behaved well I would be well-treated. My mother also said that not all men were good and that many people could be unkind and stupid. She told me that horses could not choose their masters. It made me afraid to think that perhaps one day I might belong to a wicked or thoughtless owner.

Chapter 3
Birtwick Park: A New Home

Early in May I was sold to Squire Gordon, who lived in Birtwick Park. I was very sad to leave my master, but he patted me gently and said, "Goodbye, Blackie. Work well for your new owner."

Squire Gordon's home was very large. I lived in a big stable which had four stalls and a huge window looking out into the yard. I was not tied up in my stall and this made me very happy because I could move around whenever I wanted. I could also see over the walls and into the stable yard from my clean and airy stall.

I had my first meal in my new home and when I had finished eating I looked into the next stall. There was a fat little pony. He was grey and had a thick mane and tail, a lovely head and an impudent look on his face. I spoke to him and said,

"What is your name?"

He turned and looked at me and said, "I am called Merrylegs and I am a handsome pony. Everybody likes me. Sometimes I take our mistress out in the small carriage, but mostly I carry the young ladies on my back. Are you going to live here too?"

"Yes, I am," I replied.

"Well," said Merrylegs, "I hope you are a good tempered horse and do not kick or bite."

At that moment I saw another horse's head looking over from a different stall. She was a big, chestnut mare with laid-back ears and an

angry look in her eyes. She gave me a savage glance and would not answer when I spoke to her.

Later that afternoon when she was out, Merrylegs told me about her. He told me Ginger had got her name because she used to snap at everybody. Merrylegs explained that Ginger had been treated in a cruel way by her previous owners and this had made her bad tempered. From the time she had come to Birtwick Park she had been treated with kindness by John, the groom, and Merrylegs could see a change in her. He was sure that Ginger's temper was improving.

Chapter 4
Sunday Freedom

I had a good home and I was happy, but the one thing I missed was freedom. For more than three years I had been able to run free in the meadows. But now, day after day, week after week and month after month, I had to stand in a stable night and day until my master needed me. And even when I went out, I had to be well-behaved and stand still and quiet, with a bit in my mouth and blinkers over my eyes. I had learned that this is how horses must live, but it was very difficult for me. For a powerful young horse who has lived in a large field where he could gallop full speed, with head up and tail tossed high, to stand in a stable day after day is very hard to get used to.

There were times when I could hardly keep steady when John came to take me out. I felt so full of life, but John seemed to understand what it must have felt like to be shut in a stable all day, and he would let me have a fast run for a few miles, once we had left the village.

The horses were taken to the fields on Sundays for a few hours of freedom. We enjoyed this treat. It was wonderful to run and gallop in the meadows and to feel the soft, cool grass beneath our feet.

Chapter 5
Ginger Tells Her Story

Ginger and I had a chance to talk on a day when we were standing alone in the shade of the trees. She wanted to know about my life and how I was broken in and I told her everything there was to know.

"I think," she said, "I would probably have a good temper too, if I had your experiences. But it is too late for me now."

I asked her why and then Ginger told me her story.

When she was very young, she had been taken away from her mother and put in a field with a lot of young colts.

There had been no one to look out for her and there had been no thoughtful master to care for her and show her kindness.

In the field where she lived there was a young boy who used to throw stones at the horses. Ginger did not get hurt, but one of the colts was hit in the face and scarred. When it was time for Ginger to be broken in, she was caught by some harsh men who handled her roughly and forced the bar into her mouth. They beat her with whips until her sides were sore when she tried to escape. Then she was put in a stall that was too small and very dark. Her master's son was determined to break her high spirits. He was a cruel drunkard who would make her run around the training field until she could hardly stand, if she did not do exactly what he wanted.

He worked her so hard one day that she

lay down exhausted, feeling very angry and unhappy.

He came for her early the very next morning and made her run and run around the track. The cruel man would not let her rest and, when she began to tire, he hit her again and again with his whip. Poor Ginger could bear it no longer and she began to rear up and kick.

There was a dreadful struggle, but at last she managed to throw him to the ground and gallop away into the fields. Ginger stayed there and rested for what she thought was a very long time. The flies swarmed around her in the hot sun and she became hungry and very thirsty.

At last, just as the sun was going down, a kind, old man came into the field with oats and fresh water for her. He spoke softly to her in a kind and gentle way and she let him

take her back to the stable. When she was in the stable, he brought warm water and gently bathed her wounds and, while she rested, he stood by her side and stroked her. He came to see her many times and Ginger was given to a different trainer called Job. He was thoughtful and kind and she quickly learned what was expected of her.

Chapter 6
I Hear More of Ginger's Story

When Ginger and I were next alone together, she told me about her second home.

She had been bought by a stylish gentleman after she was broken in and had gone to live in the city. Her new master pulled her reins very tight because more than anything else, he wanted to be fashionable. With the reins so tight, poor Ginger had to keep her head held high all the time. She was not allowed to move at all. The two bits which she had to wear were very sharp and hurt her tongue and made it bleed. There were times when she had to stand for hours waiting for her master. She was whipped if she moved or put her head down. This treatment was enough to drive her mad. Every day she had to put up with harsh words and beatings. Ginger wanted to make her owners proud of her and she was willing to work, but they did not care about her and only made her suffer.

Her mouth and neck became so painful that it was unbearable and Ginger would snap and kick when anyone came to harness her. In the end, when she could stand it no more, she broke free from her harness and ran away. Then she was sold and had several different owners. She did not stay long in any home because people were afraid of her bad temper. Her last home had a very rough master who poked her with a pitchfork if she did not obey. One day, she bit him on the arm when he tried to beat her with a riding whip.

After this, he was afraid to come near her and so it was that Ginger learned one way for a horse to deal with cruel human beings.

She then told me that from the time she had come to live at Birtwick, her life had changed a great deal. John and James, the grooms, had treated her with extra kindness. As the weeks passed I could see that Ginger was becoming more gentle and cheerful and that she was beginning to lose her angry look.

Chapter 7
Merrylegs Teaches the Children a Lesson

Mr. Bloomfield lived in the village with his large family. He was the vicar and he used to visit Birtwick with many of his children. They all liked to ride on Merrylegs.

One day, he had been out with the children for a very long time and, when James brought him into the stable, he said, "Well now, you had better behave yourself, or we will both get into trouble."

I was surprised to hear this and I said, "Merrylegs, what have you been doing?"

He tossed his little head and said, "I have

just been teaching those children a lesson. They do not know when they have had enough and they could not see that I had had enough, so I threw them off my back. It was the only thing they could understand."

I was really shocked to know that Merrylegs had done such a thing, but he told me that he took great care with all the children. If they were afraid and unsure, he would go slowly and steadily, until he felt them getting used to it, then he would go faster. But on this particular day, after he had been ridden for more than two hours, the boys still wanted to keep on riding him. They made whips from hazel twigs and hit him a bit too hard. Merrylegs had stopped a few times to let them know that he needed a rest. But the boys thought he was like a machine that could go on and on and on. Not for one second did they remember that he was a living pony with feelings and that he could get

tired and angry.

So when the boy on his back started to hit him on the legs, Merrylegs had picked up his hind feet and the boy had fallen off. Merrylegs loved the children very much, but he thought those boys needed to be taught a lesson. He was trusted by everyone and, in return, Merrylegs tried to be as gentle as he could with the children. After he had told me all about it, he turned and said,

"I will never kick or be bad tempered because I would be sold at once. I might find myself with a selfish owner who would work me to death, or with cruel men who would whip me. Or I could be at some seaside town where no one cared for me except to see how fast I could run. No, I will take great care that I never come to that."

Chapter 8
A Long Conversation with Wise Sir Oliver

One sunny afternoon we were all let out to graze in the orchard. I stood in the shade of the trees with an old, but very good-looking, horse named Sir Oliver. His tail was only about six or seven inches long and I had often wondered why it was so short. So I decided to ask him how he had lost his tail.

"Certainly not by accident," he snorted, "It was a wicked and disgraceful deed. I was only a very young horse when I was taken to a place where these shameful things were done. Then when I was fastened so tightly that I could not move at all, my beautiful tail was cut off, straight through the flesh and the bone."

"That is horrible!" I said quietly.

"Yes, it was a horrible thing, but it was not just the pain that made it so dreadful. It was the humiliation of having my beautiful tail taken from me. I need a tail to flick off the flies. You cannot imagine how much I am tormented by the flies which settle on my skin and sting me and now I have no way to get them off. Cutting off my tail is a wrong that can never be put right but, thank heaven, they no longer cut off horses' tails.

"Why was it done then?" Ginger asked.

"Simply for fashion!" snorted the old horse as he stamped his foot. "Fashion means that somebody got the idea in his head that horses must have their tails cut short to look smart. Surely we would have been born with short tails if God had meant us to be that way."

"And it must then be fashion that makes them force up our heads with those horrible, sharp bits that I had to wear in the city," said Ginger.

"It certainly is," Sir Oliver answered. "The idea of fashion must be one of the worst things that humans ever became involved with. As an example, look what happens to dogs. They have their ears pinned back and their tails cut off because people think it makes them look more attractive. I used to have a wonderful friend called Sky. She was a brown terrier and she slept in my stall. She had five tiny puppies and she loved them very much. Then one day a man took them away, but that night Sky found them and brought them back, carrying them one by one in her mouth. They were not the happy puppies that I knew. There was blood on them and they were crying. Part of their tails had been cut off and the soft flap on their ears had also

been sliced off. I shall never forget how frightened and upset poor Sky was and how carefully she licked their wounds. After some time, they were healed and the puppies forgot about the pain, but they had lost forever the soft flap which gave protection to the sensitive part of their ears. Why don't people cut the ends off their own children's noses, or cut their ears into points to make them look pretty? It would make just about the same sense as what they do to us."

Thinking about these things made the gentle, old horse very angry and, when Sir Oliver told me about them, I became angry too. I felt a hatred towards people which I had never felt before. I could not understand why people did such cruel things. Ginger had listened as we talked and then, with flaring nostrils and head held high, she announced that in her opinion men were fiends and boneheads.

Just at that moment Merrylegs appeared. He had been rubbing himself on the branches of an old apple tree.

"Bonehead is a very bad word," he said.

"We have to use bad words for bad things," answered Ginger, and she told him everything Sir Oliver had said. Then Merrylegs spoke, "I know it is all true, for I have seen that happen to many dogs. But we should not talk about it any more. Our master, and James and John are always kind to us so we know that there are good people in the world too. We should be thankful that we have a good home where we are well treated."

We all knew that what Merrylegs had said was true and we began to calm down.

Even Sir Oliver had to agree that he had good masters and his life here was happy. And so we ended our talk in the orchard and we began to eat the juicy apples which had fallen from the trees.

Chapter 9
Caught in a Terrible Storm

One day, my master decided that I should be given a proper name. He stroked my head and looked at me thoughtfully for quite a long time. Then he called for James and John and said, "What do you think of the name 'Black Beauty'?"

"Black Beauty certainly suits him," John said. "Yes, it is a very good name for him."

It was a wonderful name and I felt proud and very grown up.

Soon after I had been given my proper name, I had to take my master on a long journey in the dog cart and John went with him. I liked to pull the dog cart because it was very light and the large wheels rolled along so easily. It had been raining heavily and now there was a strong wind blowing the leaves across the road. We travelled along quickly until we got to the wooden bridge.

At the bridge, the gate man told my master that the river was rising fast and that he was afraid it would be a stormy night. Already, many of the fields were under water and, where the low part of the road had flooded, the water was almost up to my knees. My master drove slowly and with great care. When we came to the town I had a good rest. It took a long time for my master to complete his business and it was late afternoon before we started for home.

By now the wind was blowing very hard and I heard my master tell John that he had never been in such a terrible storm. As we

travelled along, the fierce wind howled through the trees and snapped off loose branches.

"I wish we were safely out of these woods," my master said.

"Yes indeed, sir," John said, "It would be very dangerous if a branch fell on us."

No sooner had he spoken these words when there was a loud crack and a splitting noise as a huge oak tree came crashing to the ground, ripped up by the roots. It lay across the road, right in front of us. I was terrified, but I didn't spin round or try to run away, I just stood there trembling.

"That was a very near thing." said my master, "now what shall we do?"

In reply, John said that as we were unable to drive over the tree, or around it, we should return to the wooden bridge.

It was almost dark by the time we had made our way back to the bridge, but we

were able to see that the water was already covering the middle of the bridge. My master didn't stop because he knew that this could happen when the river flooded. We were travelling along fairly quickly, but the very moment my feet were on the bridge, I realised something was wrong. I stopped and would not go forward.

"Come on, Beauty," my master said, and he touched me with the whip, but I would not move. Then he hit me quite hard but I still refused to move.

"Sir, something must be wrong," said John and he leaped down from the cart and came over to me, to try to lead me across the bridge.

"Come on, Beauty my lad, what is it?" he asked.

I couldn't tell him, but I knew for certain that the bridge was unsafe.

At that moment, the gate keeper to the

bridge ran out; he was waving a torch at us.

"Stop! Stop!" he yelled. "Don't move another step!"

"What is wrong?" my master shouted.

"It's the bridge," answered the gate-keeper. "It is broken in the middle and part of it has been swept away. You will fall in the river if you go any further."

"Thank God!" my master said. "Thank God!"

"You clever Beauty," John said, as he gently took my bridle and carefully turned me around.

The wind was calmer now and the sun had set. It got darker and darker and there was an eerie stillness in the woods. The wheels made hardly a sound as I trotted quietly along the soft, dirt road. John and my master were talking softly. They knew that I had saved their lives by refusing to cross the bridge. I heard my master say that people had the

power to reason, but that animals had special powers of their own, which often saved the lives of the ones they loved. John knew this to be true and he and the master told stories of how many horses and dogs had come to the rescue of their masters. They both understood that people did not appreciate their animals as much as they should.

So the night passed and we finally arrived at the entrance to Birtwick Park. The gardener was standing by the gates waiting for us.

He said the mistress had been so worried about us that she had stayed up all night. Then we saw a light as the hall door opened and the mistress came running to meet us. She called out,

"My dear, I have been so worried. Are you safe? Did you have an accident?"

"No, my dear. Thanks to Black Beauty, we are safe. If it had not been for him we would

all have been lost in the river," said the master.

I heard nothing more, for they went into house and I went to the stable with John. He made a thick bed of straw for me to lie on, and gave me a delicious meal. I was very grateful. The night had been very long and I was exhausted.

Chapter 10
James Howard: A Fine Young Groom

Early one December morning I had been out for my daily exercise with John. We had just got back to the stable when our master came in. There was an open letter in his hand and he looked very thoughtful.

"Good morning, John," he said. "Do you have any complaints about James?"

"No, sir, none at all," answered John. "He works hard and he is always patient and kind with the horses."

As John talked the master listened.

James was standing in the doorway. When

John had finishing speaking, the master was smiling at James.

"James, my boy, I wanted to know all about you because I have some information that could be of help to you," said the master. "This letter is from my brother-in-law. He is looking for an honest and reliable young groom who would be able to take excellent care of his horses. This job would be a very good start for you and my brother-in-law is a fair and good man.

"I know John will miss your help, but we won't stand in your way if you want to take this opportunity. Have a think about it and then tell me what you want to do."

A few days later James decided to leave us and go on to the new job. Meanwhile, he needed more practice in driving, so the carriage was taken out more times than I had ever known. Ginger and I pulled the carriage and James practised his driving skills.

He drove us in the city. I liked the smells of the coffee, tobacco and bread which came from the open shops and it was fun to see all the other horses and carriages. James was becoming a good driver and Ginger and I were having a very good time.

Chapter 11
The Stable Fire

My master and mistress had some friends
who lived about forty-five miles from Birtwick.
One bright afternoon, they decided to visit
them and James drove the carriage. On the
first day we travelled for thirty-two miles.
There were many long hills on the journey,
but James was a careful and considerate
driver. He made sure that we didn't get too
tired. He remembered to put the brake on
when we went downhill and to take it off
when it wasn't needed. Once or twice we
rested on the way and we got to the town

where we were to stay the night, just as the sun was setting.

When we came to the large inn in the middle of the market place, we went under an archway and stopped in a long yard behind the inn. There were stables and coach houses at one end and two men came out to meet us. Ginger and I were led into the stables, and James watched the men to see that they made us clean and comfortable.

Later that evening, I was resting in my stall when I heard a horse being brought into the stable. There was a young man smoking a pipe. He was talking to the grooms while they cleaned the horse. One of them asked him to put out his pipe and give the horse some hay. I heard him pass by my stall and throw the hay on the floor. Then they locked the stable door and went away.

Some time later, I woke up feeling very uneasy. I didn't know what time it was or

how long I had been asleep. The air was so thick it was hard to breathe. Ginger was coughing and I heard another horse moving about in his stall. I couldn't see anything at all, it was so dark, but I could smell the smoke in the stable.

Then I heard a crackling and a spitting sort of noise coming from a small trapdoor which had been left open. I started to shake all over. I was very frightened. All the other horses were awake now and they were afraid too I could hear them pulling at their halters, snorting and kicking and stamping.

Then I heard a different sound. Someone was coming! A man burst into the stable with a lantern in his hand. It was the groom who had brought the last horse in. He ran from stall to stall untying the horses and trying to lead them out. But he was in such a great hurry, and seemed so afraid himself, that I became more frightened than ever. The first

horse he tried to lead would not move, nor would the second or third. Then he came to drag me out but I was too scared to go with him. He tried all the horses, but none of them would move, so he gave up and left us.

Perhaps we were stupid not to leave the stable, but we didn't know what was happening and there was no one there for us to rely on. It was much easier to breathe now that fresh air was coming in through the open door. The spitting, crackling sounds above my head were getting louder and on the stable wall a red light flickered.

"Fire! Fire!" someone shouted and then I heard a soft and soothing voice. It was James.

"Wake up, my beauties, come with me, it is time for us to go."

He came for me first because I was near the door. He stroked my head and said,

"Let's get your bridle on, Beauty, and we'll be out of here in no time."

I followed him out of the burning stable, out of danger and into the safety of the yard. He told someone to stand with me while he went back for Ginger. I gave a loud whinny as he ran back into the stable. Ginger told me later that I had done a good thing by whinnying so loudly. She had heard me in the yard and it had given her the courage to leave her stall.

The yard was noisy and chaotic, with people shouting and rushing about in every direction. Some were leading horses out of the other stables. Thick smoke was pouring out of the stable where James had gone. I was watching it closely when I heard my master shouting,

"James! James! James Howard! Where are you?" But there was no reply. Only the noise of things crashing down in the fire could be heard. Then I saw him! I let out a happy, deafening neigh as James led Ginger out

through the smoke. She was coughing badly and James couldn't talk at all.

"You brave, brave lad!" my master said, and he patted him on the shoulder. Then he asked him if he was all right, but James could only nod his head, for he still couldn't speak.

That very same night, we left the town. We were all feeling sad. James had told us that the stable roof had fallen in and that the horses which could not be led out in time had been buried under the burning rafters.

Chapter 12
A Sad Farewell to James

The second part of our journey seemed very easy after our terrible time at the fire and we arrived at our destination just before nightfall. We were led into a clean, warm stable and we were made very comfortable by a kind coachman. When he heard about the fire he spoke to James and said,

"Young man, it is very clear to me that your horses know whom they can trust and depend on. When there is a fire or a flood, it is one of the most difficult things in the world to get horses out of their stable."

After three days at this place, it was time to go home. We had no problems on our return journey. John was delighted to see us all back safe and sound and we were happy to be home and in our own stable.

That night John and James were talking about a young boy called Joe Green. We heard them say that when the time came for James to leave Birtwick Park, Joe Green was to take his place. He was only fourteen years old, but John said that he was a clever boy and willing to learn.

We saw him for the first time the very next day. He was at the stables to learn as much as he could before it was time for James to leave. He learned how to carry the hay and straw and how to sweep out the stable. James had to teach Joe how to groom on Merrylegs because he was too small to reach up to Ginger and me. Merrylegs was not at all pleased about this, and called him a 'child

who knew nothing'. But after two weeks, even he had to admit that Joe Green was a quick learner who would do very well.

On the day that James had to leave us, he seemed quite miserable, but he tried not to let it show. He told John how much he would miss the horses he had grown to love so dearly and also his family and friends. John tried to cheer him up by telling him that his family would be proud of him in his new job and that he would soon make new friends.

We were all very sad to see James go. Merrylegs was so upset that he wouldn't eat for several days. Every day, John let him out in the fields so that he could gallop around until he began to feel happy again. James had been our very good friend. He had always treated us with particular kindness, and we found it hard to believe that we would never see this good man again.

Chapter 13
A Race Against Time

It was late one night, not long after James had left. I was fast asleep on my bed of straw when I was startled by the sound of a bell; it was very loud and I was wide awake at once. I heard John running to the hall. After two or three minutes he was back and he quickly unlocked the stable door and said,

"Come on, Beauty! Now you must run as fast as you can."

Almost before I had time to think, John had put my saddle and bridle in place and I was being led up to the hall. I could see the butler standing by the door with a lamp and he said,

"Our mistress is very ill; her life is in danger. There is no time to lose. Ride as quickly as you can and give this note to Dr. White. Make sure that the horse has a rest at the inn, then come back as soon as you can."

When we got to the road, John said quietly,

"It is time for you to do your best, Black Beauty. Our mistress's life depends upon it."

When I heard these words, I knew what I had to do. I galloped along the road as fast as I could. I had been running for two miles when we reached the bridge. John stroked my neck and pulled gently on the reins to slow me a little.

"You have done well, Beauty," he said. "Now take it easy for a while."

But I could not slow down: my spirit was up and I galloped on as fast as before.

We arrived at Dr. White's house at three in the morning. John banged on the door and rang the bell until, at last, the doctor came to the window to see what he wanted. John told Dr. White that our mistress needed him immediately because she was very ill. We waited at the door until he came down.

He was there in a few minutes and John gave him the note. Then Dr. White asked if he could ride back to Birtwick on me because his own horse was ill. John knew I was too hot and also very tired, but he knew how important it was for the doctor to be with our mistress.

The journey back home was not easy for me. Dr. White was quite elderly and did not ride very well. But I did the best I could and we soon arrived at Birtwick Park. Joe was at the gate, waiting for us. The doctor went into the house with my master and I went into the stable with Joe. I was thankful to be home for

I was gasping for breath and my legs were shaking. My whole body was wet and steaming. Joe got a cloth and rubbed my chest and my weary legs, but he did not put my warm blanket on my back. He thought I was far too hot to want a blanket on me. He brought me some corn and hay and gave me some cold water. Then he closed the stable door and left me for the night, thinking he had done all the right things to make me comfortable. It was not long before I began to feel very cold and I started to shiver and shake. My legs ached, my chest was sore and I hurt all over. How I wished for my blanket and for John to come, but I knew that he would still be walking back from the doctor's house, so I tried to sleep as I lay in the straw.

It was a long time before John arrived at the stable. I was in so much pain that I could only make a low moaning sound. He was quickly at my side and, although I couldn't

tell him, he seemed to know at once how I felt. He put two or three warm blankets over me and then ran to get some hot water from the house. I heard him say under his breath that Joe Green was a stupid boy for not putting my blanket over me, or giving me warm food to eat and warm water to drink.

I was desperately ill. There was a severe infection in my lungs and every breath I took was painful. John stayed with me day and night to nurse me. My master came to see me every day.

"My poor Black Beauty," he said, "you are the one who saved the mistress's life and now you are ill yourself."

I felt proud that I had saved the mistress's life and I heard John say that in the whole of his life he had never seen a horse run as fast as I had.

It took a long time, but eventually I began to feel better. The horse doctor had come several times with medicine and this had helped to get rid of the infection.

John continued to be angry with Joe Green for quite a long time but, in the end, he could see that the boy hadn't meant to hurt me. He just hadn't known the right things to do.

Chapter 14
We Leave Our Happy Home

After I had been in my happy home at Birtwick Park for three years, I had a feeling that something very sad was going to happen. We had known for some time that our mistress was ill. Our master looked worried and sad and the doctor had been coming to the house several times a week. Then we heard the dreadful news. The doctor said that our mistress needed to move to a warm climate for a few years and she must leave as soon as possible. Our master made all the arrangements for the move as quickly as he could and everyone in the household was miserable.

John did his work, but he said very little and rarely smiled and Joe didn't talk at all. Ginger and I soon learned where our next home would be. Our master had sold us to an old friend who he believed would be a good master. The local priest had wanted a pony, so the master gave Merrylegs to him, but he did it only on the condition that Merrylegs was never to be sold and, when he could work no longer, he was to be shot and buried.

The day came for the master and mistress to leave Birtwick Park. Ginger and I brought the carriage up to the hall door for the very last time. Rugs and several household items were brought out by the servants and, when everything was organized, the master carried the mistress down the steps and into the carriage. Then he turned to the servants and said goodbye and thanked them all for their

loyal service.

We travelled to the railway station at a slow pace and when we finally arrived the mistress said,

"Goodbye and God bless you, John. We will always remember you."

John made no reply, but I felt the reins tremble and I knew that he was unable to speak. When everything had been taken out of the carriage, John went on to the platform and Joe came to stand by us. He put his face close to our heads to hide his tears. Poor Joe! How sad he was! It wasn't very long before the train came into the station. After a little while, the doors closed, a whistle blew and the train pulled away. It was soon out of sight.

When John came back, he said, "They have gone! We shall never see them again – not ever."

We left the station with heavy hearts and, with Joe beside him, John drove back to Birtwick Park.

Chapter 15
Earlshall Park

After breakfast the next day, it was time for us to leave. Merrylegs whinnied from across the yard and Joe came to say goodbye. John put the leading rein on me and the saddle and bridle on Ginger. Then he rode us to our new home, Earlshall Park.

When we got there, John asked to speak to Mr. York. It was a long time before he came over to meet us. He had a stern voice and was dressed in fine clothes. He took a quick look at Ginger and me, then a groom took us into the stable. It was light and airy and we were put in stalls next to each other. After about half an hour, Mr. York came in with John and they talked about us. Mr. York wanted to know if we had any bad habits or any particular likes or dislikes. John told him that we worked well as a team and that we would work hard if we were looked after well and treated in a kind way. He also told him about Ginger's hard life and warned that she would go back to her bad-tempered ways if she was treated badly. As they were leaving the stable, John paused and said,

"I think you should know that we have never used the check-rein with either of these horses. The dealer told us it was the gag-bit that ruined Ginger's temper. The black horse has never had one on."

"I prefer a loose rein myself," said York, "and the owner is also considerate of the horses. But unfortunately his wife has different ideas. Whenever she goes out in the carriage,

she insists the horses are reined tightly. She wants to be fashionable, so at this place, they will have to wear the check-rein."

"I am very sad to hear this," John said, "but please take good care of the horses and try to treat them with kindness."

Then John came to us and he whispered kind and loving words to us. His voice trembled and he sounded very sad.

I didn't know how to say goodbye. I just put my face close to him. In a few seconds he was gone and I was never to see him again.

Our new owner seemed to be quite pleased with us when he came to see us the next day. Mr. York told him what John had said about the check-rein. He listened thoughtfully and said that he understood. However, as his wife insisted upon the tight rein being used, Mr. York must get us used to it a little at a time.

Ginger and I were harnessed and put to the carriage the following day. The mistress

came out; she was tall and dressed in beautiful clothes. She looked at us and seemed irritated by something, but she got into the carriage without speaking.

It was uncomfortable wearing the check-rein because I found that I could not put my head down when I wanted, but at least it did not pull my head higher than I had been used to. Ginger was steady and quiet, but I was concerned about her.

The next day, we were again harnessed and put to the carriage. Our mistress came out and said,

"Mr. York, I do not like the way those horses look. Put their heads higher."

He tried to explain that we were not used to a tight rein, but she told him to make the reins tighter.

It wasn't long before I came to realise that all the awful stories I had heard from other carriage horses were true. As each day

passed our reins were tightened more and more until I began to dread having the harness put on. Pulling the carriage uphill was hard for us. We had to pull with our heads raised up and this was very painful. It made our legs and our backs ache so badly that my spirit began to weaken and Ginger was becoming more and more unsettled. She hardly spoke at all.

For the past few days there had been no more shortening of the rein and I thought the worst was over. But it was yet to come.

Chapter 16
Harsh Treatment

One afternoon, our mistress came out later than usual for her daily ride. There was an angry look on her face and York was ordered to strap our heads up even higher. He came to me and fixed the rein so tightly that my head was pulled back to an almost unbearable position. Ginger realised that he was going to do the same to her and she began to jerk her head up and down. York managed untie the rein in order to shorten it and at that moment, Ginger reared up so unexpectedly that he was hit on the nose and the groom was almost knocked to the ground. Immediately they tried to steady her, but Ginger kept on rearing and kicking and flinging herself about. In the end, she plunged over the carriage pole and fell. She may well have done more damage had York not held her head down to keep her from struggling.

Then the groom managed to release me from Ginger and the carriage and I was taken back to the stable. A little while later, two other grooms brought Ginger in. She had many knocks and bruises. York came to inspect both of us and he seemed to be very distressed by what had happened. He grumbled about a world in which fashion was more important than living things and wished that he had refused to shorten the rein. As soon as Ginger's wounds healed, one of the master's sons wanted her as a hunter, so she was never put on the carriage again.

I still had to pull the carriage, but now I

had a new partner.

It would be impossible to describe the pain I suffered with that rein for four endless months. If it had gone on much longer my health and temper would surely have given way. The pulling of the sharp bit on my tongue and my jaw made my mouth foam and the unnatural position of my head put pressure on my windpipe and made my breathing very painful. By the time I got back to the stable I was worn out, my chest and neck ached and my mouth and tongue were sore. I felt depressed and full of despair.

In my old home, John and the master had always been my friends, but here I had none. York must have known how I was suffering, but he did nothing to help me.

Chapter 17
Left in the Care of Reuben Smith

Sometimes York had to go away on business. On these occasions he left a man called Reuben Smith in charge of the stables. Reuben Smith was a kind and gentle man, who knew how to look after horses properly, but he also had a problem. There were times when he drank too much and, when he was drunk, he was unreliable, his behaviour was a disgrace and he was a nuisance to everybody. York knew about the problem but he decided that Reuben could be trusted because he had promised that he would not touch another drop of alcohol while he was in charge of the stables.

The family was expected to return to Earlshall Park some time in May and it was one day at the beginning of April that Reuben was sent to the town to run some errands. I had to pull the carriage. We went at a steady trot and when we got there a groom took me to a stable to be fed and to be rested before the journey home.

I could feel a loose nail in one of my front shoes, but it wasn't noticed by the stable groom. Reuben came back to the stable a few hours later. He said it would be at least another hour before we left for home because he wanted to spend some time with some old friends who were also in the town. Some time before this, the groom had noticed that I had a loose nail in my shoe and he asked Reuben what he should do about it.

"Do nothing," said Reuben, "I will see to

it when we get home. It will be all right until then."

I was very surprised when I heard Reuben say this, because he had always been so concerned and careful about these things in the past. He spoke in a loud and angry way and seemed to be in a very bad mood. Then he went away.

Reuben came back at about nine o'clock that evening and it was quite clear that he had had too much to drink. It was still very dark when we began the journey home. We had not even left the town when Reuben put me into a gallop along the stony roads. At this fast pace my loose shoe soon came off. I'm sure that had Reuben not been drunk he would have noticed this straight away and slowed me to a walk. Instead, he drove me on still faster and faster until my foot started to throb with pain. The sharp stones had cut the underside of my hoof and the sides were split

and broken. It was impossible to go on; the pain was just too much for me to bear. I stumbled very badly and fell down on my knees with such great force that Reuben fell off me. I heard a loud thud as his body hit the ground. I soon struggled to my feet and managed to limp to the side of the road. By this time the moon had risen and I could see Reuben lying in the middle of the road. I could hear him groaning, but he was very still. I was in great pain so I just stood by the road and waited in the quiet, April night. I thought of the times long ago, when I used to lie in the cool meadow, with my mother at my side.

As I stood and listened for the sound of horses, or wheels, or footsteps, my pain grew worse. How I hoped that help would come soon.

Chapter 18
Tragic Consequences

Time passed slowly and it must have been around midnight when I heard the sound of a horse's feet as it trotted down the road. I thought I recognised Ginger's step and I let out a loud neigh when I was sure it was she. The carriage came slowly now and stopped when it reached the dark figure that lay motionless on the ground. One of the men jumped down and knelt beside Reuben. After a moment or two, he said,

"He's dead. His hands are cold. I am afraid Reuben is dead."

Reuben's hair was soaked with blood and there was no sign of life when the two men lifted him up. After they had laid him down again, they came to look at me. They saw that my knees were cut and my foot was badly damaged. It did not take them long to work out what had happened, or to realise that Reuben had brought about his own death by drinking too much.

In a little while, we started the sad journey home. I was in great pain as I limped slowly back to the stable. When I got there, my foot was washed and bandaged and wet cloths were wrapped around my knees. In spite of the terrible pain, I managed to lie down in the soft straw and sleep. The horse doctor came to examine my legs the next day. He said that my wounds would heal in time, but that my knees would always be scarred. They tried their best to cure me, but it was very painful. The scar tissue on my knees was

burned out with a strong ointment. After it had healed, a blistering lotion was put on the front of both knees to take all the hair off. I don't know why they did this, but they must have had a reason.

An inquest was held because Reuben's death was very sudden and there were no witnesses. The innkeeper was able to testify that Reuben was very drunk that night and that he had ridden out of town at a very fast gallop. My lost shoe had been found among the stones, so the cause of death was quite clear and I was not to blame.

Chapter 19
Brought to Ruin and Sold Again

I was turned out into a small field as soon as my knees had healed. I enjoyed the sweet grass and the freedom, but I was very lonely because there were no other animals with me. I missed Ginger very much because we had become such good friends. When I heard horses passing by on the road, I often whinnied, but I seldom got an answer. Then, one day, Ginger was brought to the field and I whinnied with joy as she trotted towards me. But I soon learned that she had not been put in the field as a companion for me. It would take too long to tell her story, but it ended with Ginger breaking down, ruined by hard riding. Now she was in the field to see what a little rest and freedom could do for her.

Sadly, Ginger looked at me and said, "Life is hard for us. Here we both are, ruined in the prime of life."

Even though we both knew that we were not the same as we used to be, we enjoyed each other's company. We no longer galloped about or played as we once did, but spent the days eating fresh grass and standing in the shade of the trees with our heads close together.

Ginger and I had been together for some time when our master came back from a long trip. He walked into the field with York and they inspected us very carefully. Our master seemed very disturbed.

"An old friend let me have these horses

because he thought they would have a good home with me. But now I see they have been ruined. However, we will keep Ginger here for a few more months and then see what she's like. But the black one will have to be sold. It is a great pity, but I will not have knees like that in my stable." The master was persuaded to sell me to a man York knew, who would treat me well and would not mind my scarred knees.

I went to another town by train. My new stable was warm and comfortable, but it seemed rather small after what I'd been used to. There were many horses and carriages which my new owner rented out. Sometimes they were driven by his own men and at other times they were driven by the ladies and gentlemen who hired them.

Before coming to this place, I had only ever been driven by people who knew how to drive. But here, it was different, for all sorts

of people drove me. On one occasion, a man and his family rented me. As we set off he jerked the reins and, even though I was going at a good fast trot, he hit me several times with the whip. A loose stone got stuck in my front hoof, but this man didn't notice. He was too busy laughing and talking. Any good driver would have realised that something was wrong after I had gone just a few paces, but we travelled more than half a mile before he noticed that I was lame. The stone was picked out of my bruised hoof by a kind farmer who had stopped us on the road. While I was rented out as a job horse, I had many painful experiences such as this.

Then one day, after weeks and weeks of this harsh use, I was hired by a gentleman who drove me with great skill. It was a relief to be driven so well and I could tell that he liked me, so I did my best for him. It was just like old times and I was happy.

After that day, he came several times and tried me with the saddle. He was looking for a safe and gentle-natured horse for a friend of his to ride. That summer my master sold me to Mr. Barry.

Chapter 20
A Thief Steals my Food

Mr. Barry, my new master, was a business-
man who lived by himself in a small house.
His doctor had advised him to take up
horseback riding. My master hired a man
named Filcher to be my groom and I lived in
a rented stable near the house. My master
treated me well, even though he didn't know
much about horses. He ordered oats, crushed
beans and bran and plenty of the best hay. I
thought I was very fortunate when I heard my
master order all this food. For three or four
days all was well.

Filcher kept the stable clean and I was washed and brushed. But after a time, I began to realise that there was something not quite right with my food. I had the beans and bran, but I knew that I was not getting enough of the oats. After a few weeks there was a change in me. I became weak and dispirited, but, of course, I could not tell anyone what was happening to my food.

The months passed and I was surprised my master didn't see that something was wrong. Then one afternoon he rode me into the country to visit a friend. This friend knew a lot about horses. He looked me over and said,

"Your horse doesn't look too well to me. I don't like to say this, but I think he has not been eating properly."

My master told him that only the best food had been ordered for me. They thought about it for a while and then my master

realised that something must be happening to my food. Had I been able to speak, I would have told my master about the oats. Every morning my groom would arrive with a small boy who carried a covered basket. They would put some of my oats into a bag and then the boy would put them in his basket and go home.

It was one morning, about a week after my master's visit to his friend, when a policeman came and caught the boy just as he was leaving the stable. The boy looked very scared and tried to shout out, but the policeman made him show where my oats were stored and how he filled his basket each morning.

It did not take long to find Filcher and then both he and the boy were taken away. Some time later I heard that the boy was set free, but Filcher was jailed for two months.

Chapter 21
For Sale at the Horse Fair

My master hired a new groom after Filcher had gone. At first the new man looked after me well enough and seemed a suitable person to take care of me. But as the days passed, he began to neglect me more and more. He rarely took me out for my exercise and often my stable wasn't cleaned for weeks. Standing in a wet and dirty stable soon caused a bad infection in my hooves.

After such bad experiences with his two grooms, Mr. Barry decided that keeping a horse was too much trouble.

After a few days I was taken to a horse fair to be sold. Although a horse fair may be enjoyable for people, it is very grave business for a horse. I had to stand with two or three other horses who were about the same size and build as I was. A lot of people came to inspect us.

They all did the same thing. First my mouth was pulled open to check my teeth, then they looked at my eyes, then they felt all the way down my legs. Some of the people did all this in a gentle way and spoke kindly to me and patted me, but others were very rough and careless with me.

One of the men who looked at me was small and well-built; he had kind, grey eyes and he spoke to me in a soft and gentle voice. I hoped he would buy me. He said he would pay a good price for me but his offer was not accepted and when I looked round, he had disappeared. The next person to look at me

was a fierce-looking man with a harsh voice. I was scared he would buy me, but fortunately he went away. Two or three other men came but no offer was made. Then the fierce-looking man returned and started to bargain for me. At that moment, the kind, grey-eyed man came back and I put my head close to him. He stroked me gently and offered the salesman a much higher price than the fierce-looking man. The money was paid at once and I had a new master. He led me away and gave me some oats and after a while we set off for home. It was a long ride, but eventually we stopped at a small house. My owner gave a whistle, the door opened and a young woman and a little boy and girl came running out to greet us. Soon they were all patting and stroking me and talking to me in gentle voices. It felt wonderful to be in this place!

Chapter 22
I Become a City Cab Horse

Jeremiah Barker was my new master's name, but everybody called him Jerry. His wife was called Polly and she was a good-looking woman with shiny, dark hair and deep brown eyes. Their two children were a boy of twelve and a girl called Dolly who was eight years old. I had never seen such a loving family.

Jerry had a cab which he drove in the city and I was to pull the carriage with Captain, his other horse.

Polly and Dolly came to visit me on the

first morning in my new home. They wanted to make friends and brought me bread and apples. It felt good to be petted and talked to again. They both said I was a very handsome horse and were puzzled as to how my knees had been so badly scarred.

Later that day, Jerry put me into the cab for the first time. He took great care to see that collar and bridle fitted perfectly. I did not have to stand with my head held too high because there was no check-rein. Jerry showed me off to the other cab drivers; he was very proud of me. Some of them said that there had to be something wrong with me because I was such a good-looking horse. But Jerry just patted my neck and smiled.

My first week of pulling the cab was very difficult because I was not used to all the traffic and the noise in the city. But I quickly learned that I could trust Jerry and gradually I became used to the noise and bustle of the

busy streets.

Jerry and I very soon got used to each other and he looked after Captain and me very well indeed. He gave us good food and our stables were always kept clean and made comfortable for us. Being a cab horse was hard work, but Sunday was a special time for Captain and me, because it was our rest day. We became good friends and I began to feel like my old self again. I was happy in my new home.

Chapter 23
Jerry Barker: A Kind and Thoughtful Master

My new master was a kind and good man. I had never known anyone like him. He always stood up for his beliefs, but because he was so good tempered, he rarely had a quarrel with anyone. The one thing that could make Jerry angry was people who asked him to beat the horses to make them run faster, just because they were late starting their journey.

One day two rowdy, young men staggered out of an inn and shouted to Jerry,

"Come here, Cabby, and be quick about it! We are late. We will reward you well if you can get us to the station in time for the one o'clock train."

Jerry said that he would take them, but only at a safe pace and for the usual fare. After thinking about it for a moment or two, the men climbed into the cab.

The city streets are always busy in the middle of the day and it is difficult to drive fast. However, it is surprising what a good driver and a good horse can do when they work so well together. When we put our minds to it, there was no-one who could beat Jerry and me at getting through the crowded streets. It was particularly difficult this day, but Jerry drove with such skill that we got to the station at least five minutes early. The two young men were very pleased.

"Thank goodness we have made it in time," one of them said, "and our thanks to you, my good friend, and your fine horse. You will never know how much this means to us."

The men tried to give Jerry more than the regular fare, but he refused to take it and helped them to get their luggage down from the cab. Jerry couldn't help wondering what was so important about that particular train, but it felt good to have helped the two young men.

When we got home that evening Jerry told Dolly and Polly about the two young men and our skilful drive through the busy traffic. Then Dolly and Polly patted and stroked me as they thanked me for getting Jerry and the men to the station safely. Jerry brushed me with great care and gave me warm oats to eat.

Chapter 24
I See Poor Ginger for the Last Time

One day, Jerry and I were waiting outside one of the parks with many other cabs. After a few minutes, a scruffy old cab, pulled by an old and worn-out chestnut mare, drove up beside us. The horse was in poor condition, she was very unsteady on her legs and her ribs were showing through her dirty, ill-kept coat. A wind blew some of the hay I had been eating towards her and she stretched out her long, thin neck to pick it up. Then she turned to look for more and I could see the hopeless look in her dull eyes. I was just thinking that I had seen her before, when she stared at me and said, "Is that you, Black Beauty?"

Yes, it was Ginger! But she had changed so much! Her once clean limbs were badly swollen and the joints had grown out of shape from too much hard work and I could see the pain and suffering in her face.

She came closer to me and began to tell me all that had happened since the time we were together in the field. Ginger told me that after a year's rest she had seemed fit enough to return to work and had been sold to a new master. For a short time all had gone well for her but, sadly, after a particularly long, hard gallop, her old injury had flared up. She was rested for a while and then sold again. She had had several more owners before she was finally sold to a man who kept horses and cabs to rent out.

"When they realised my weakness was permanent, they complained that I was not

worth the money they had paid for me and said I was to be put on a small cab and used until my strength gave out. This is what they are doing to me. I am whipped and worked without even a Sunday rest," Ginger said sadly.

"In the past, when you were badly treated you used to stand up for yourself," I said.

"Yes, I did at one time," she said. "But now I know it's no use, for men are stronger and, if they are cruel and have no feelings, there is nothing we can do about it. We must suffer until we die. I can't bear another day of this terrible life. I wish I was dead now."

I was overcome with sadness and could think of no words to comfort her. I put my nose close to hers and she seemed pleased to see me. She spoke again,

"Black Beauty, you are the only friend I have ever had."

At that moment her driver arrived. He

gave her a sharp pull on the mouth as he backed her out of the line and drove away. Soon after this, a cart passed with a dead horse in it. It was a horrible sight! I saw a chestnut head with a white streak down the forehead, hanging out of the cart and blood was dripping from the tongue. I think it was poor Ginger. At least her troubles would be over. I think it would be kinder of people to shoot us before we come to such misery and suffering.

Chapter 25
Goodbye to a Loving Family

Although holidays such as Christmas and the New Year may be very happy times for some people, horses and cab drivers do not think so. They have to work long hours because there are so many late-night parties. It is not unusual for a driver and horse to wait for hours in the pouring rain or freezing cold until the people inside have finished their celebrations.

In the Christmas week there was a lot of work for us and Jerry was not well; he had developed a terrible cough. Polly was worried about his health and she always waited for us to come home, no matter how late it was.

On New Year's Eve at about nine o'clock, we had to take two fine-looking gentlemen to a house in a city square. They said we should return at eleven o'clock to pick them up, but as it was a party, they might be a few minutes late and we were to wait for them.

We were at the door as the clock struck eleven. We heard it chime every fifteen minutes until it was midnight, but still they did not come out.

A strong wind blew cold, hard sleet in our faces and Jerry climbed down from the cab to pull my blanket further up my neck. There was nowhere to shelter from the icy winds or the driving sleet and rain and Jerry was now coughing very badly indeed.

The two gentlemen finally came out of the house at quarter past one and, after telling

Jerry where to drive, they climbed into the cab. I was afraid I might fall because my legs were numb with cold, but we arrived at our destination safely. These men did not even say sorry for having kept us waiting. In fact they were very annoyed because they had to pay Jerry extra money for the long wait.

Jerry could hardly speak by the time we got home and his cough was much worse. I could see that Polly was very concerned about him but she said nothing. Even though he was very tired, Jerry rubbed me down and gave me some warm food and made me as comfortable as he could.

When morning came, it was Jerry's son who came to the stable and cleaned and fed us. I could sense that there was something wrong for he was very quiet. Then Polly came to the stable later that day and she was crying as she talked to her children. I heard her say that Jerry was dangerously ill and it

was possible that he might die.

We waited anxiously for news of him and a week went by before I heard Polly say that Jerry was out of danger. As the days passed Jerry's health began to improve, but the doctor told him that he could never return to the cab work again. It was soon after this that a letter arrived for Jerry and Polly. It was from an old friend who lived in the country. She had written to tell them they could have an empty cottage, which was very near her own home, and Jerry could work for her as a coachman. The children would be able to go to the school nearby.

After talking about it for a little while, it was decided that they should move to the country as soon as Jerry was well enough. The cab and horses would have to be sold as quickly as possible.

I was very sad to hear this news because I loved my home and my master. I was growing

older and even though it was hard being a cab horse, I knew I did my work well.

Jerry would not let me be sold for cab work. I was to go with a good friend of his, who would find a new home for me.

When the time came for me to leave, I did not see Jerry because he was still not allowed to go outside. But Polly came with the children to say goodbye to me. She whispered sweet words as she stroked and petted me. She said that she wished I could go with them, then after a few minutes, she put her arms around my neck and kissed me. As I was led away to my new home I could still feel her gentle touch.

Chapter 26
Heavy Loads: I Grow Weaker

My new owner was a baker and corn dealer Jerry knew him and he believed I would have a comfortable home and that my work would not be too hard. This would have been the case, but unfortunately my new master was not always there to oversee his workmen. The foreman at the stable was always shouting and rushing about and forcing everybody to work faster and harder. There were many times when he made my load too heavy for me to pull easily. Jakes, my driver, told him that it was too much for me, but the foreman took no notice of him, because Jakes was only a worker.

I had to wear a check-rein again in this new job and I began to lose my strength after about four months of pulling such heavy loads. One day I was given a heavier load than usual and we were on a road with a steep uphill climb. I pulled with all of my strength as I tried to get up the hill, but it was impossible and I had to rest. Jakes got angry and began yelling at me.

"Go on, get a move on, you lazy horse, or I shall hit you with my whip!" he yelled.

Then he started to whip me. Again and again I felt the sharp leather cut into my soft flesh and, just as I began to think I could bear it no longer, a woman's voice said,

"Please stop that at once! Do not hurt your fine horse again. Can't you see that he is trying his best for you? He can not use all of his weight against the collar while that check-

rein is fastened so tightly."

Luckily for me Jakes took the old woman's advice and my rein was loosened. Now that I could get my head down I could use all of my power and, with one final great pull, I managed to drag the load up to the top of the hill.

Then the old woman crossed over the road and came to me. She stroked my face and patted my neck and it was a good feeling to be treated kindly again. She told Jakes that he must never forget how hard it is for a horse to pull such a heavy load uphill with a check-rein and he should not use it any more. Jakes nodded to her and from that day on he gave me a loose rein. But my loads were still too heavy for me and I grew weaker as the days passed.

After my day's work I was kept in a stable with no daylight and this almost destroyed my eyesight. Every day I became more disheartened and miserable.

Chapter 27
My Misery and Suffering Become Unbearable

The more depressed I became, the more my health and strength deteriorated and before long, I was sold again. I had become too weak to do my share of the heavy work.

My new master was a cab owner. He was a cruel-looking man named Nicholas Skinner. There was an evil look to his face. He had a hooked nose and black eyes and his mouth was twisted and unsmiling. When he spoke his voice was harsh and grating.

People often say that seeing is believing, but for a horse it must be that feeling is believing.

Until this time in my life I never knew the absolute misery and suffering a cab horse has to endure.

Nicholas Skinner was the owner of several run-down cabs and the men who drove them were very poor drivers. The men were hard on the horses because Skinner was hard on the men. Every day we were made to work long hours in the blazing heat of the summer sun and there was no Sunday rest.

From time to time, a group of men would arrive on a Sunday morning and I had to take them for a drive in the country. They always told my driver to make me run up and down the steep hills as quickly as I could. At the end of these rides I was always too exhausted to eat and could only pick at my food. How I wished that Jerry was there to give me a tasty, bran mash! I also thought how much easier my work would be if I had a Sunday rest. But

there were no rests and no nourishing food in this place. I had a driver who was just as ruthless as Skinner. He often drew blood when he hit me with his vicious whip and sometimes he would strike me about the head and flick the lash under my belly. Treatment such as this made me feel that it was not worth being alive. I remembered my days with Jerry and his family and I missed their gentle care and kindness. But in this place, no one cared about my feelings and I was treated as if I were a machine.

Life had now become so wretched for me that I often thought of poor Ginger and, I too, wished that I was dead. And that wish almost came true.

On this particular day I had started my work at eight o'clock in the morning. I had already done several rides when a man asked to be taken to the railway station. We got him there in good time for the train and then we

waited around because my driver thought we might get some more business. After a while a family of four came over to us; they wanted to be taken into town with all their heavy luggage. As the father was loading the cab, a little girl approached me, looked at me and then called out,

"Father, come and see this poor horse. He looks worn out and I am sure he is too weak to take us and all our luggage."

"He is a lot stronger than he looks," my driver said. "Don't you worry yourself about him, miss."

The girl's father hesitated, but my driver was so anxious to have the fare that he began loading the cab with the heaviest pieces of luggage and then he piled on more and more bags until the cab springs were straining.

I had been out since early that morning and I had had no rest or food but I tried my best to pull that heavy load in spite of all the evils

men had done to me. I was doing quite well until we reached a steep hill but it was too much for me. I was exhausted but struggled to keep moving as my driver hit me again and again with his cruel whip. Suddenly, I felt my feet slip from under me and I crashed to the ground. My strength had all gone and I lay motionless. I thought I was going to die. There was noise and chaos all around me and I could hear angry voices as the luggage was being unloaded. I heard a child say,

"It's all our fault! That poor horse! What have we done to him?"

It all seemed like a dream. But I was aware of someone loosening the strap of my bridle and undoing the collar. Then a voice said, "I think he is dead. He won't get up again." I was gasping for breath and I did not open my eyes, but I could hear a policeman telling the others what to do. Somebody poured some liquid down my throat and someone else

splashed cold water over my head. Then a blanket was spread over me as I lay on the cold, hard street.

After some time I began to recover. There was a kind man at my side, comforting me and urging me to get up. I tried once or twice and then I lurched to my feet and stood there shaking. When I was steadier, I was gently guided to some nearby stables to rest and to have some warm food.

By that evening, I was well enough to be taken back to Skinner's stables. He came to see me the next morning.

"This horse is finished," he said. "He needs six months' rest before he can work again. But I won't waste time and money on sick horses. I'll sell him for as much as I can."

I was given plenty of food and I rested for ten days. Mr. Skinner wanted me to look my best for the horse fair.

Chapter 28
Saved by Farmer Thoroughgood and His Grandson

At the horse fair I was put with a lot of other broken-down horses. Some of them were just old, but others were lame or broken-winded. Some were in such a poor state that it would have been kinder to shoot them.

There was a poor-looking crowd of buyers and sellers. Some were trying to find buyers for their worn-out animals and others were trying to buy ponies and horses for hardly any money at all. These were hard men, made hard by hard times! I felt afraid and how I wished that I could hear a friendly voice again.

As I looked around me, I saw a young boy standing by the side of a man who looked like a farmer. The man's shoulders were rounded, but his back was broad, and he wore a wide-brimmed hat. He had a kind face and I saw his eyes begin to sparkle when he saw me. I lifted up my head and pricked up my ears as I looked at him.

"Look, Willie, my boy, I can see that this horse has known better days," he said. "He must have been something very special in his younger days."

He patted my neck in a kind and gentle way and I stretched my nose out towards him. The boy rubbed my face and said,

"Oh look, Grandpa, you can see that the poor old chap understands kindness. You made Ladybird young again and you could do the same for him. Please say you will buy him."

"Ladybird wasn't an old horse. She had been badly used and she was just run-down," his Grandfather replied.

But the boy persisted and said that maybe I too wasn't that old, that I too was just worn out and that all I needed was a good, long rest.

The farmer smiled at the boy and ran his hand down my legs to check their condition. They were still bruised and swollen. Then he looked at my teeth and he could see that I was not so very old. I was bought for a small amount of money and led away from the fair by the boy and his Grandfather.

Willie's Grandfather was a farmer; his name was Mr. Thoroughgood. He said that Willie was to take care of me. I had oats and hay every morning and evening and, during the day, I was taken to a field where the sweet grass grew. Willie gave me carrots and spent hours by my side stroking and petting me.

BLACK BEAUTY

I began to improve. My legs had healed and by the middle of spring I was able to take Willie and Mr. Thoroughgood to the town in their fine carriage. They were happy and proud of me. They talked about my future and decided that I must be found a good home where I would always be cherished and loved.

Chapter 29
I Find a Loving Home

It was summer and one day the groom took extra care when he cleaned and brushed me. My coat shone in the sunlight and I knew that I was looking my best. I could sense that my life was about to change. Willie chattered excitedly as he and Grandfather got into the carriage.

"I am sure the ladies will like him," the old man said, "and if they do, they will be happy and so will this brave horse."

After we had travelled about two miles we came to a small house by some trees. Willie jumped down from the carriage and rang the bell. The door opened and three ladies came out. They were smiling and seemed very excited to see me. One of the ladies said at once how much she liked me. Her name was Miss Ellen. They asked a lot of questions about me and Mr. Thoroughgood told them all about the bad treatment and overwork that I had suffered. He said that I was now in excellent condition and only needed a home where I would be treated with love and kindness. They talked about it and decided to keep me for a trial period to see how things worked out. Willie and his grandfather hugged and patted me as they said goodbye.

I was taken to my new stable and given some warm food. A groom came by and stood and stared at me.

"Black Beauty had a star on his face just like you, old fellow," he said, "and he was the same height as you too." There was a tiny

mark on my neck from an injection that I had been given many years ago. When he saw this he started muttering to himself in amazement.

"The white star on the face, the white patch on the back and the one white foot. You must be Black Beauty! Oh Beauty! I am Joe Green. Can you remember the boy who years ago nearly killed you by forgetting to cover you with a blanket on that freezing night?"

Joe hugged and patted me and I felt safe and happy so I touched his cheek with my nose to show that we were friends. Joe was overcome with joy.

After this we went out almost every day because Miss Ellen and her two sisters liked to drive out in the carriage with me.

I have been in this wonderful place for a year now and Joe is the best and the most caring groom that I have ever known. I grow stronger every day. Willie and Mr. Thoroughgood often come to see me and the three sisters have promised that I will never be sold. All my troubles are over and I am home at last.